Follow Me
To The Beach

This book is for my angels, Brance, Baileigh, Jake and Karli. Nothing would be possible without God's grace and blessings, and the inspiration and support from: my little co-pilot Brance, you gave me the reason to write a book about our favorite hobby, my Travis for being the "Wrangler" in my life, and my best friend and co-author for believing in me and encouraging me to follow my dreams. I could not have done this without you.
- Melissa Neel

To my precious little boy Brooks and his love for all things with wheels and an engine, and for my darling little girl Ellorie who's sugar, spice and everything nice, but she's not afraid to get dirty! I thought of you both every step of the way-this is all for you.
For my dear friend Melissa who's excitement and drive motivated me to follow through with the project. What a treasure to embark on this journey with you. Thank you for the push.
- Christi Jones

To my brilliant son Mason. You inspire me.
- Nathaniel P. Jensen

D1318459

"Hey Wrangler,"
"I'm headed to the beach,
wanna come along?"

"Sure do!"
"What should I bring?"

"Grab your tools because you never know when you might need them," says Verdi.

"Shouldn't we take a map so we won't get lost?"

"No way! Follow Me, I know a shortcut. We can get there in half the time with more time to play."

"Sounds good to me, I'm right behind ya!" shouts Wrangler.

"The beach is just on the other side of this mountain," explains Verdi.

"Verdi, WATCH OUT for that fallen tree!"

"Where's your sense of adventure?"
Verdi asks.
"We can make it over that. No problem!"

"Yee haw! Go for it!"
cheers Wrangler.
"Now wait for me, here I come!"

"You can do it Wrangler."
encourages Verdi.

"Wrangler, what's wrong?"

"We have a problem. I think a branch from that tree over yonder punctured a hole in my tire."

"Hold on little buddy, let me get your tool kit. We can patch this up and be on our way in no time," says Verdi.

"Don't ya think this is a little too steep Verdi?......I'm 'fraid I'll roll down the mountain."

"Just make sure you're in a low gear, and take it slow," cautions Verdi. "We're almost there...you're doing great!"

"Wrangler?"

"Yah, Verdi?"

"Can you hear that? .... listen."

"Waves... I can hear waves.
We made it. Yee haw!"
Wrangler hollers with
excitement.

"Let's see how far we can go until the waves wash over our hood!" shouts Verdi.

"Great idea! Last one in's a rotten humzee!" squeals Wrangler.

"WAHOO, hold on to your seat, here come the waves!"

"Verdi, what's that?"

"What? I don't feel anything."

"Yuck! You have sea weed on your roll bar," eeewww don't get it on   me..........
aaahhhggg gross get it off, get it off!"
whines Wrangler.

Woosh, Splash, waves come crashing
down washing away all of the sea weed.

"Hey, let's refuel" Verdi says to Wrangler.

"Sounds good to me, I think I just might be runnin' on empty."

"Hey Verdi, who's that?"
As Verdi looks back, "We've got company!"

As Verdi approaches the other trucks, "Hey, you all are a mess. Where have you been?"

"There's a great mud hole around the corner. Do you want to play with us?" the other truck asks.

"SURE DO! Verdi, let's go!"

"Verdi, can ya do this?" asks Wrangler as he drives around and around in circles.

"You bet I can!"

"Hey Verdi, you alright?"

"Blaaaaaa.....I don't feel so well."

"Awwww. Looky there...what's the matter little guy? I guess you're not quite big enough to handle this mud hole," teases the other truck.

"Don't listen to him. We both know you're not little!"

"You're right," Verdi replies, "but it still makes me sad to be made fun of. That wasn't nice at all. We were supposed to be having fun playing together in the mud."

"I'm sorry ya feel sad Verdi. How' bout we run through the waves one more time to wash off all this mud and then we'll head back home."

"Wrangler, you're much more fun to play with. That other truck was really mean. It's not nice to make fun of others."

"Yah, I know whatcha mean. Besides, we're all different.

Some of us are big, some small, some green, and some blue." says Wrangler. "That's what makes us all unique and special."

"Let's not play with mean trucks ever again," says Verdi.

"I think that's a good idea. Are ya ready to head on back home?" asks Wrangler.

"I guess so. The ride to the beach was fun! Thanks for coming with me," says Verdi.

"You betcha! I can't wait to go on more adventures together."

61108910R00020

Made in the USA
Lexington, KY
01 March 2017